WIDE-AWAKE WESLEY
by TONY GARTH

Wesley was always wide awake.

He did anything he could to avoid going to bed.

"I'm not tired," he said, at bedtime.

He always found a reason to stay up late, and later, and later...

Any excuse would do.

Perhaps there was something on TV?

"Can I just watch the end of this programme about basket weaving in Outer Mongolia? It's brilliant," he said.

Or,

"Can I just finish this jig-saw puzzle? It won't take long," said Wesley, putting the very first piece on the table.

Or,

"I'm just finishing my supper," he said, taking the tiniest bite possible from a big piece of toast.

His excuses got worse and worse.

"Mum, I can't go to bed. There's a great big hippopotamus in my wardrobe," he said, one night. "I'm much too scared to sleep."

But Wesley's favourite trick was to lie in bed and shout.

"Mum, Mum, I'm thirsty. Can I have a glass of water, please?"

As soon as he'd had one glass, he wanted another. And then, of course, he had to keep getting up to go to the toilet.

This usually went on for some time.

It was Christmas Eve. Wesley lay tucked up in bed, wide awake as usual.

"I'm going to stay awake until Santa arrives with my presents," he announced.

"Now, Wesley," said his Mum, "Everyone knows that Santa won't bring you any presents until you're fast asleep."

Wesley wasn't listening. He sat up in his bed, eyes open wide, and waited...and waited...and waited.

Outside, on the roof, sat a large, jolly figure dressed all in red, with a fluffy white beard. It was Santa Claus. And he was waiting for Wesley to fall asleep so he could pop down the chimney and deliver his presents.

Santa waited...

And Wesley waited...

Morning came and still Wesley was wide awake. So, of course, he didn't get any presents. Not one. In fact, no one got any presents that Christmas because Santa was still waiting on Wesley's roof.

All over the world, children woke up to find their Christmas stockings empty. And it was all Wesley's fault.

Wesley's picture was in all the newspapers, as the boy who spoiled Christmas Day. He felt terrible.

"Wake up, sleepy head," said Wesley's Mum's voice. "It's Christmas Day. Don't you want to see what Santa has brought you?"

Wesley woke up, with a start. There at the end of his bed was his Christmas stocking. And it was brimming with presents!

"Thank goodness," he said. "It was only a dream. Santa did come after all."

Wesley never forgot his Christmas dream. He made his Mum a promise.

"From now on, I promise always to go straight to sleep," he said.

"On Christmas Eve, at least," he added, in a whisper.

Look out for the next twelve Little Monsters!

FRIENDLY FRANCO
CLUMSY CLARISSA
BOISTEROUS BILLY
SICKLY SIMON
SERIOUS SADIE
GROWN-UP GABBY
PERFECT PRUDENCE
RUDE ROGER
DANGEROUS DAVE
CURIOUS CALVIN
DIRTY DERMOT
TANTRUM TABITHA